AR level: 4.9
AR points: 0.5

Spanish

AR level: 3.2
AR points: 0.5

eng.

BLAZERS®
Bilingüe/Bilingual

Monstruos extintos/Extinct Monsters

El lagarto destripador gigante

Giant Ripper Lizard

por/by Carol K. Lindeen

Traducción/Translation: Dr. Martín Luis Guzmán Ferrer

Consultor en lectura/Reading Consultant: Barbara J. Fox
Reading Specialist
North Carolina State University

Consultor en contenidos/Content Consultant: Dr. Richard Gillespie
Visiting Fellow, Department of Archaeology and Natural History
Australian National University, Canberra

Capstone
Press

Mankato, Minnesota

Blazers is published by Capstone Press,
151 Good Counsel Drive, P.O. Box 669, Mankato, Minnesota 56002.
www.capstonepress.com

Library of Congress Cataloging-in-Publication Data
Lindeen, Carol, 1976–
   [Giant ripper lizard. Spanish & English]
   El lagarto destripador gigante / por Carol K. Lindeen = Giant ripper
lizard / by Carol K. Lindeen.
   p. cm. — (Blazers. Monstruos extintos = Blazers. Extinct monsters)
   Text in Spanish and English.
   Includes index.
   ISBN-13: 978-1-4296-0608-0 (hardcover)
   ISBN-10: 1-4296-0608-8 (hardcover)
   1. Megalania — Australia — Juvenile literature. 2. Mammals, Fossil —
Australia — Juvenile literature. 3. Paleontology — Pleistocene — Juvenile
literature. 4. Paleontology — Australia — Juvenile literature. I. Title. II. Title:
Giant ripper lizard. III. Series.
QE862.L2L5618 2008
567.9'4 — dc22   2007031427

Summary: Simple text and illustrations describe Megalania, how they lived,
   and how they became extinct — in both English and Spanish.

Editorial Credits
Jenny Marks, editor; Ted Williams, set designer; Jon Hughes and Russell
   Gooday/www.pixelshack.com, illustrators; Wanda Winch, photo researcher;
   Katy Kudela, bilingual editor; Eida del Risco, Spanish copy editor;
   Danielle Ceminsky, book designer

Photo Credits
Courtesy of Steve Bourne, 29 (skeleton)
Shutterstock/EcoPrint, 8–9 (landscape); Glenn Jenkinson, 4–5 (Australian
   outback); Jiri Vondracek, cover (forest marshland); Ronald
   Sumners, 6–7 (Australian outback)

1 2 3 4 5 6 13 12 11 10 09 08

Table of Contents

Tabla de contenidos

Wild Australia/ La Australia salvaje

A million years ago, strange animals roamed the earth. Many huge creatures lived in Australia's wild, wooded grasslands.

Hace un millón de años, por la Tierra merodeaban animales muy extraños. Muchas de estas gigantescas criaturas vivían en las praderas boscosas y salvajes de Australia.

A monstrous lizard ruled Australia. This fierce beast was called the megalania.

Monster Fact

The giant ripper lizard's full name is Megalania prisca. The name means "ancient giant butcher."

Datos sobre el monstruo

El nombre completo de este lagarto destripador gigante es Megalania prisca. El nombre significa "antiguo carnicero gigante".

Un monstruoso lagarto mandaba en Australia. Esta bestia feroz se llamaba Megalania.

Large and In-Charge/ Grandote y mandón

The megalania was an enormous meat-eater. This monster weighed about 1,300 pounds (590 kilograms).

El Megalania era un carnívoro enorme. Este monstruo pesaba cerca de 590 kilos (1,300 libras).

Ripper lizards grew up to 20 feet (6 meters) long. These giants were longer than a full-sized pickup truck.

El lagarto destripador alcanzaba 6 metros (20 pies) de largo. Estos gigantes eran más largos que un camión de carga.

The megalania had thick, powerful legs with pointed claws. Its sharp, curved teeth were jagged like saw blades.

Megalania's sharp claws/
Las filosas garras del Megalania

12

El Megalania tenía unas patas gruesas y poderosas con garras puntiagudas. Sus dientes, filosos y torcidos, eran mellados como la hoja de un serrucho.

Monster Fact

A strong ripper lizard could have killed animals 10 times its own weight.

Datos sobre el monstruo

Un lagarto destripador fuerte podía matar animales 10 veces más pesados que él.

The megalania had excellent eyesight. Even from far away, it could spot a moving animal in an instant.

El Megalania tenía una
excelente vista. Aunque se
encontrara muy lejos, podía
distinguir al instante a un
animal en movimiento.

Scientists think ripper lizards laid eggs. They probably buried the eggs and left them to hatch.

Los científicos piensan que los lagartos destripadores ponían huevos. Probablemente los enterraban y se marchaban.

A Deadly Killer/
Un asesino mortal

A hunting megalania took its prey by surprise. The lizard used its sharp teeth and long claws to rip its dinner to shreds.

Cuando cazaba el Megalania tomaba a su presa por sorpresa. Este lagarto usaba sus filosos dientes y sus largas garras para hacer trizas a su cena.

This monster also ate dead animals it found. A megalania could smell a rotting body 7 miles (11 kilometers) away.

Este monstruo también se comía a los animales muertos que se encontraba. El Megalania podía oler un cuerpo en estado de descomposición a 11 kilómetros (7 millas) de distancia.

Giant kangaroos were probably one of the lizard's main meals. But a hungry megalania could catch and kill animals as big as a rhinoceros.

Probablemente los canguros gigantes eran uno de los principales alimentos del lagarto. Pero un Megalania hambriento podía matar animales tan grandes como un rinoceronte.

Megalania Disappears/
El Megalania desaparece

When humans settled in Australia, they came face to face with this monster. The rule of the megalania would soon come to an end.

Cuando los seres humanos poblaron Australia, se encontraron frente a frente con este monstruo. Pronto el poder del Megalania llegaría a su fin.

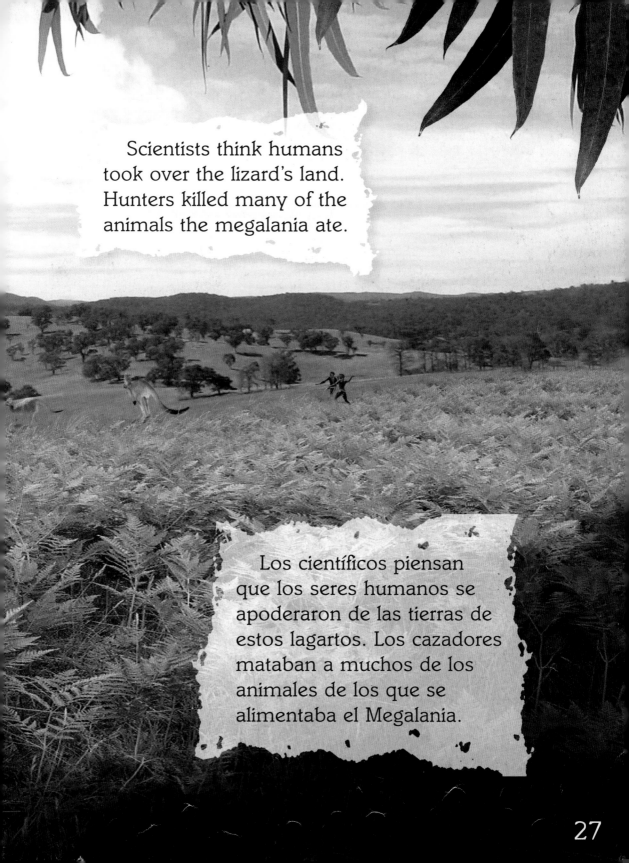

Scientists think humans
took over the lizard's land.
Hunters killed many of the
animals the megalania ate.

Los científicos piensan
que los seres humanos se
apoderaron de las tierras de
estos lagartos. Los cazadores
mataban a muchos de los
animales de los que se
alimentaba el Megalania.

The megalania became extinct 40,000 years ago. Its fossils have been found in eastern Australia, but they are rare. No complete skeletons have been discovered.

El Megalania se extinguió hace 40,000 años. Sus fósiles se han descubierto en el este de Australia, pero es raro encontrarlos. No se ha descubierto ningún esqueleto completo.

Monster Fact

Scientists think the Komodo dragon and the Australian perentie lizard might be relatives of the ripper lizard.

Datos sobre el monstruo

Los científicos creen que el dragón de Komodo y el lagarto de perentie pueden ser los parientes más cercanos del lagarto destripador.

Glossary

enormous — extremely large

extinct — no longer living; an extinct animal is one that has died out, with no more of its kind.

fossil — remains or traces of an animal or plant that lived long ago

jagged — sharp and uneven

monstrous — large and frightening

powerful — having great strength

prey — an animal that is hunted by another animal for food

shred — one of several torn-up pieces or strips

skeleton — the framework of bones that supports and protects the body of an animal with a backbone

Internet Sites

FactHound offers a safe, fun way to find Internet sites related to this book. All of the sites on FactHound have been researched by our staff.

Here's how:
1. Visit *www.facthound.com*
2. Choose your grade level.
3. Type in this book ID **1429606088** for age-appropriate sites. You may also browse subjects by clicking on letters, or by clicking on pictures and words.
4. Click on the **Fetch It** button.

FactHound will fetch the best sites for you!

Glosario

enorme — extremadamente grande

el esqueleto — armazón de huesos que sostiene y protege el cuerpo de los animales con columna

extinto — que ya no vive; un animal extinto es aquel que ha desaparecido y del que ya no quedan ejemplares de su especie.

el fósil — restos o vestigios de un animal o planta que vivieron hace mucho tiempo

mellados — filosos y desiguales

monstruoso — enorme y aterrorizador

poderoso — que tiene mucha fuerza

la presa — animal que es cazado por otro animal para comérselo

triza — uno de varios pedazos o tiras desgarrados

Sitios de Internet

FactHound te brinda una manera divertida y segura de encontrar sitios de Internet relacionados con este libro. Hemos investigado todos los sitios de FactHound. Es posible que algunos sitios no estén en español.

Se hace así:

1. Visita *www.facthound.com*
2. Elige tu grado escolar.
3. Introduce este código especial ID **1429606088** para ver sitios apropiados a tu edad, o usa una palabra relacionada con este libro para hacer una búsqueda general.
4. Haz un clic en el botón **Fetch It**.

¡FactHound buscará los mejores sitios para ti!

Index

Índice